Love rage

John Ashworth (1963-) was born in Lancashire and educated in Nigeria, Liverpool, Stonyhurst College and Cambridge University.

He subsequently lived and taught in Kent, Kenya, Bath and Argentina before working in a medium secure psychiatric hospital for ten years.

He currently works in Cambridge University and lives in Cambridge with his family.

Love rages, life wanes.

I write
For there is a calling,
Some cloaked distant
Figure on a hilltop
Standing in the rain
Waving to me.

And the words
Tumble down,
Falling from old wardrobes,
Some bright,
Some dull,
Some with musicality.

I cannot rest
Until the words
Are spoken,
Or at least
Have moved
Along.

Love rages, life wanes.

In the middle
Of my heart
A deep lake lingers
Surrounded by trees,

Night fishermen sing
Their songs of
Comfort and
Belongingness.

Unlimited the sky,
A charcoal black.
The boats wait
To return home,

Whilst we swim
In the warmth
Of the water
In the light of
The stars

Where I whisper
Words of love.

Love rages, life wanes.

Under the shade of a tree
In some mid-European place
With my hat and my dog
My madness begins.

It is a grain of unfortunateness
Playing upon the truth
Falling beyond
The power of my caring

For it is certain that I will
Never know the beginning
Or the end and I will lose
The thread of understanding.

For all is my love,
For I wished to be loved,
For I wanted love's tenderness
I cannot speak.

I cannot find a place
For me nor speak something
That a man would

Understand.

Instead, I count the clouds
And count the people
Who did not stop to talk to me
To see the madness in my eyes.

I cannot raise my voice; I'm silent,
My body finished, a rage of desire
That made this place so unfortunate
So, I am bleak and rested here.

Beneath this tree I spy the shadows
As the shadows fall upon me
In my life, in my quietness
To see what has become of me.

Love rages, life wanes.

There is nothing dishonorable
About dying young,
Though the children's feet
In their play
Have stampeded the blood
Of the immature cockerel
That had not found his voice
And was surplus
To requirement
(Though the colour
Of his feathers
Were promising).
Their feet then washed
In the river
Sending coral water
To the sea
And the sun shone
Another day
On the trees
Where the chickens
Roosted.

Love rages, life wanes.

The smell of barbecuing
Meat fat hangs in the air
Like an overused kitchen towel

Whilst swallows dive-bomb
In between the cars
As old, old men
In too many clothes
Walk to the bakery.

Unoccupied balconies
Are too full of sun
And the piazza's fountain
Is just a trickle.

Old chewing gum
On the pavement
Is loosened
And the traffic
Has become stationary.

Love rages, life wanes.

In the afternoon
When the sun streams
I am in the shadow
Of my mind
Counting dreams
Whistling in the dance
Of some fortune
Embracing hope,
Tabulating light,
Seeing in blue and red
Tasting the orange,
The dust of my life
For the dust has settled
All around me, in between
The grass and the tree
And the blaze
Of my horizon
Through the waters
At my fingertips
And the wetness
Of my eager lips.

Love rages, life wanes.

I could have
Caught that moment
And stored it
For myself.

Your kiss,
A spoken word,
Your hair
Encroaching on
My silent, lonely
Self.

I never told you
I was anything
More than I am
A blank picture
Torn up in colours
That you see
But I can't.

A trail of sandy
Horizons bitten
By harsh frost

Love rages, life wanes.

Or the shadow
Of a sun
That left me
Gasping for breath.

I told you
Things
About myself
And repeated
Phrases
Around some scores
Of adventures
Whilst the seabirds
Circled above
The madness
I have endured
Though quietly cooked
In my life.

I do not project
My love as much
As I would like.
Love rages, life wanes.

Love rages, life wanes.

Got a head shaped
Like a cannelloni bean
No sex, even on Sundays
And no alcohol to drink.

Keep fit diets
Language restricted
On profanities,
Clothes unrelaxed.

Bristles profuse
Like thistles in ears,
Dark patches in nostrils,
Runaway eyebrows.

Back a-hump,
Knees groaning,
Hips winging,
Stomach singing.

Suburban atheist,
Liberal humanist
Drinks tepid tea

And dreams

Of willing dusky types
In tropical settings
And sleep and rice
And pineapple chunks.

Love rages, life wanes.

My wife spits fire
And coconut and shrapnel
Drawing blood into her lungs,
Exploding all traffic
Covering the sun
With her palm,
Evaporating lakes,
Re-arranging forests.

She is mine though
And at quarter past seven
We are watching a film
Together in bed,
Drinking tea and smoking.

Her face, spectacled,
Is a kind horrendous monster.
Horizontal we watch.

Love rages, life wanes.

Whilst the dogs sleep
And the song of bells
Rains heavily
I wonder if I am god.

Though believing in nothing
I am absent from understanding
Happiness in its complexity
Running out of thinking.

Like flowers the sun plays on
My canopy of thinking
And the slow weave again
Begins the fat bellied
Yellow snake.

Entering my mind
Declaring my perilous
Future
Of doomed anxiety.

Drowned in dim, green light
The thunderous cascade

Of mouth open and closing
Like a fish. The water is cold.

Love rages, life wanes.

Sandied I am from the beaches
Of Sardinia trailing grains into places
To eat beef, artichokes and risotto,
To admire the dark waitresses.

The sun casts a strange shadow
As I walk, like from a bedside lamp
Through the fields full of flowers
As the sheep bells chime their song.

My mind is as happy as I can allow
As all I see, taste and smell
Is fine and no one can cut it down
And leave me to live in starvation.

But you with your hair the colour
Of wheat
And the lines of dissatisfaction
In your face
Bring all to sorrow.

You mourn too much
What you might and might

Love rages, life wanes.

Not have and your body
Wrestles the moment
Between awake and nightmare.

Amongst our interaction
There is only a void
And no kisses or a word
That would warm
Our situation.

We are lost
In our childish acceptance
Of sadness
Without prospect.

In my calling to you
It is as if you are
On the other side
And do not hear
Because of the wind.

Love rages, life wanes.

You will soon be a woman.
Already your childish ways
Have gone,
You saunter like a bird,
So smooth your direction.
Your face glows,
Your face shines.
I remember your sweet
Gummy smile - that first tooth,
Your first day at school,
Your first friends,
The day you cried
When you knew
All things die
(So sweet is your nature).
Now into the grown-up world
You belong,
People listen to
Your stories,
Your laugh is infectious,
Your cry and tears
So desolate.
You are your mother's girl

(Though I gave you strength).
She gave you softness.
So proud am I
Of the woman
You will be.

Love rages, life wanes.

Love plays no part
In my daily contemplation,
Only life which is a curve
Delimitating all those people
Caught like a glimmer between
Rest and activeness,
And me, I will stare into
A trance and move nothing
Until some thought will lift me
Into action, but until then
I will be here in despair
Trapped in my desire to sleep
Everything completely away.

Love rages, life wanes.

I saw two girls,
One after the other
In the smell of coffee.
I asked the first;
'Are you American?
Are you Australian?'
Irish-accented, full of that
Vaguely disoriented hope
People have when they have
Dropped out, or a disease
Which is life-long.
Full of rampant prettiness
So close to fields
And showers of rain.
The other served a beer,
Gold skin, whistling.
Happy whilst I write this,
Thinking of things I
Can do with my life.

Love rages, life wanes.

Watching the leaves
In the wind.
Drinking coffee
In a thick jumper
Silent.
Procrastinating
Procrastinating.
Always in a worry
Of some self-made
Manufacture,
Unless I am cooking
Or eating, or drinking
(Something that will
Calm me down).
It is not anxiety
(For that is worse
In its perpetual state).
But a slight edginess
That is not quite real
Or physical
That gnaws at me,
Ruins my blood,
Raises my heartbeat.

Love rages, life wanes.

Bring on the spring
As sunlight does
Bring relaxation!

Love rages, life wanes.

My woman
From Buenos Aires
Has slim
Elegant hands.

Her earlobes
Are allergic
Except to gold
And her blood group
Is A-positive.

This senorita
Loves life,
Loved me
Or anything
That will love her.
She is a magnet
For love.

I am bound
To observe
Her vitality
Dream something

Of her aspiration

She sings a song
Of hope and passion
And I sit and watch
Whilst I teach her English
With my drawings.

She is not mine,
Though sometimes
I want her, and lie beside her
And talk in the afternoons.

Love rages, life wanes.

I have two daughters,
One brown-eyed and pretty
With a face like honey melon
And a quiet resolute way
Like a bird in flight.
My blue-eyed daughter
Shines like a saint
Her wit matches mine!
I sit, as if a king
Amongst my princesses
Though the presence
Of these people
Forces me to be respectful.
Respectful through song,
Silence and beauty.
I am allowed the presence
Of their bodies,
To hear their sweet chatter
And to be privy to their games.
Nothing gives me more pleasure
Than my presence with them.

Love rages, life wanes.

Awakenings repair the jigsaw
To those who suffer mental strife
Despite the shifting
Of the coastal sands.

Like the kite of mind that bobs
Its way into the valleys
And the heights
My way has no fastening

And my soul
Is lost in a vast cavern
With no decisive path.

My words of self-expression
Grow like tortuous spines and spikes
Their purpose denied create distaste,
In unharmonious, unwelcome poison.

And anyway, reaching out is nil
For those who could restore me
Are intellectually self-entrapped,
I am thus alone.

Love rages, life wanes.

Early winter
Fastens leaves.
I dream I could sketch
In charcoal - but like
My way of inadequate speech,
Poorly representing myself,
I prefer to be quiet
As someone experienced in life.
Enough to let beauty
Pass without comment.
In the face of you,
In these legal lights,
I can only be astonished.

Love rages, life wanes.

In the point
Between the trees,
The sand and the water
There lies the body
Of my loved one,
Partially bruised by
The probing fingers
Of the undertakers,
Silent and foreboding.
The breeze falls heavily
On her eyelashes
And the rose of her lips
I once kissed
Have blanched.

Love rages, life wanes.

I fell in love with the legs
Of the woman
Crossing the bridge
And the ears of the
Taiwanese serving drinks.

Through the stockings
Of the receptionist
And the heels in the lift,
I bounder like
Some closet Jesuit priest.

I did not want so much
And I did not want
So little, just wanted to idle
Passing the time.

Love rages, life wanes.

In Unakulwa village
The Kookooranga bird
Wakes me at night
To listen to the hum
Of a sole mosquito.

Deadened I am and dirty
From the Kandy train,
Teeth still full of snacks,
Feet sore from the vibration
Of the Diesel engine.

Before sleep
I was full of rotty pancakes
And twelve flavored tiny
Dishes of curry I had,
Then I ate a bowl
Of honeyed curd.
My body believed
Paradise had come.

In the morning I drink tea,
Fawn coloured,

Love rages, life wanes.

Bitter-sweet, eat thick coins
Of sweet banana with passion fruit
And survey the day.

Later, digesting, the tuk-tuk
Speeds me away to Tangalla
For entertainment, lunch later on
And any occupation that will
Carry me to siesta time.

For then love,

You
Lie damp
In this Sri-Lanka air
And although I am quiet
I remember you.

You gave us two
Beautiful children,
Fed them like birds,
Raised them to be dashing
Intelligent creatures.

Love rages, life wanes.

You listen to my recounts,
My perceptions of life,
Full they might be.
When my mental baboons
Escape and tear down
The traffic signs of life
You find a quiet place
For me to reassemble the jigsaw.
You are my guardian.

You seem to suffer little
Disappointment when
We have little yet
All around is silver and gold.

We grew from children
Ourselves my loved one
And have had many adventures
Some cruel, some kind.
But together we have
Always been!

Love rages, life wanes.

He chases me
With the light and shadows
And his premonition
And humor
Tests my will,
Tempting me with tasks
That I can never do
But am charged
To see the light.
He has starved me
Of sleep,
Removed my desire
To eat or drink,
Burnt me with water
Too hot for bathing.
My endurance for this
Disappoints, disappoints.
He is not of human form,
But speaks from the sun.

I am forced to be an instrument
To his will,
Erased, dehydrated,

Love rages, life wanes.

But I take the tasks.

And then I smoked
But the smoke disliked me,
I split it into two
But the core of the light
Was still burning
So I spat on it,
But it did not extinguish
And my spit dangled
The fire with three knots
In it.
A bird told me to swing it
And I did.

At 5pm in the afternoon
Clouds, grey-luminescent
In our courtyard,
I sat on the animal throne,
A beam of light centralised me
And in a natural action
I offered my throat, resigned to death
If need be.

Love rages, life wanes.

I say willingly:
'Take me, for I am happy to die
If it is your will for I love you.'

God the strict, the kind,
Empathetic with a wicked
Sense of humor and
A tendency to forget.
So sometimes I do not want
This life,
It drives me to despair.
They see my tears
But do not understand
My position.

Love rages, life wanes.

In those silent moments
Between the bridges of busy time
I give my prayer to a god somewhere
Yet there is no answer.

This refusal forces sadness
And I am a boy again, embarrassed
In the field of the world,
Uncertain of myself.

How can I make a place
For my heart and my head
To bring to life my dreams
To grow to be a man?

In moments all security I have built
Is dampened down with the fear
That darkness will win
And all the sunshine and green
Of happy times will only be a memory.

Printed in Great Britain
by Amazon